little bee books

An imprint of Bonnier Publishing Group

853 Broadway, New York, New York 10003

Copyright © 2015 by Elina Ellis

First published in Great Britain by Templar Company

This little bee books edition, 2015.

All rights reserved, including the right of reproduction in whole or in part in any form.

LITTLE BEE BOOKS is a trademark of Bonnier Publishing Group, and associated

colophon is a trademark of Bonnier Publishing Group.

Manufactured in China 0515 024

First Edition 2 4 6 8 10 9 7 5 3 1

Library of Congress Control Number: 2014957615

ISBN 978-1-4998-0109-5

www.littlebeebooks.com

www.bonnierpublishing.com

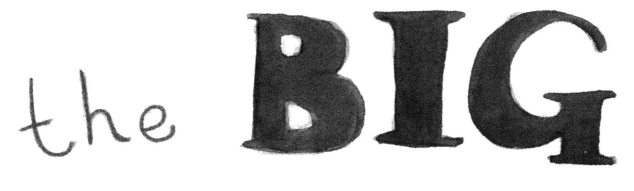

the BIG Adventure

Elina Ellis

little bee books

It was the start of a new day. Moose, Fox, Chicken, and Bear stared out of the window and wondered what to do. "Let's go beyond the hill and have a really BIG adventure," said Bear.

"But a really **BIG** adventure needs a lot of planning and preparation," said Moose. They all agreed.

"Let's go to Africa!" said Fox.

"Or the North Pole!" said Bear.

"We could go to the moon," said Moose.

"Or to the next village," said Chicken. "My auntie lives there."

"I would love to see a whale," said Bear.

"Or a lion," said Fox.

"Or an alien," said Moose.

"Or my auntie," said Chicken.

They started to pack.

"We'll need these," said Fox.

"And these,"
said Moose.

"And we can't go without these,"
said Bear.

"Are you sure we need all that?"
asked Chicken.

Then they began to worry.
"What if there is a STORM?"
said Moose.

"Or a fire?" said Bear.

"Or a crash?" said Fox.

"Don't worry," said Chicken. "Everything will be okay."

The night before the big adventure,
nobody could sleep.

"I am so excited!" said Moose.

"I'm nervous," said Fox.

"My tummy feels funny," said Bear.

Chicken said nothing.

In the morning, the four friends
checked their map...

and climbed up the hill.

The other side of the hill looked beautiful!

And so did the little village where
Chicken's auntie lived.

"How far is it to Africa?" asked Fox.

"How about the North Pole?" asked Bear.

"And the moon?" asked Moose.

"They are a long, long way away," said Chicken.

"But the village where my auntie lives is right there!

Let's go there first!"

So they ran down the hill toward the village.

"This isn't as scary as going to Africa," said Fox.

"And not as cold as going to the North Pole," said Bear.

"Or as far as the moon," said Moose.

"And if we hurry, we will be just in time
for lunch with my auntie," said Chicken.

"Well, this BIG adventure is fun!" said Moose.

"We are very brave!" added Fox.

"And adventurous!" said Bear.

"We might go even farther next time," said Chicken.

And they all agreed.

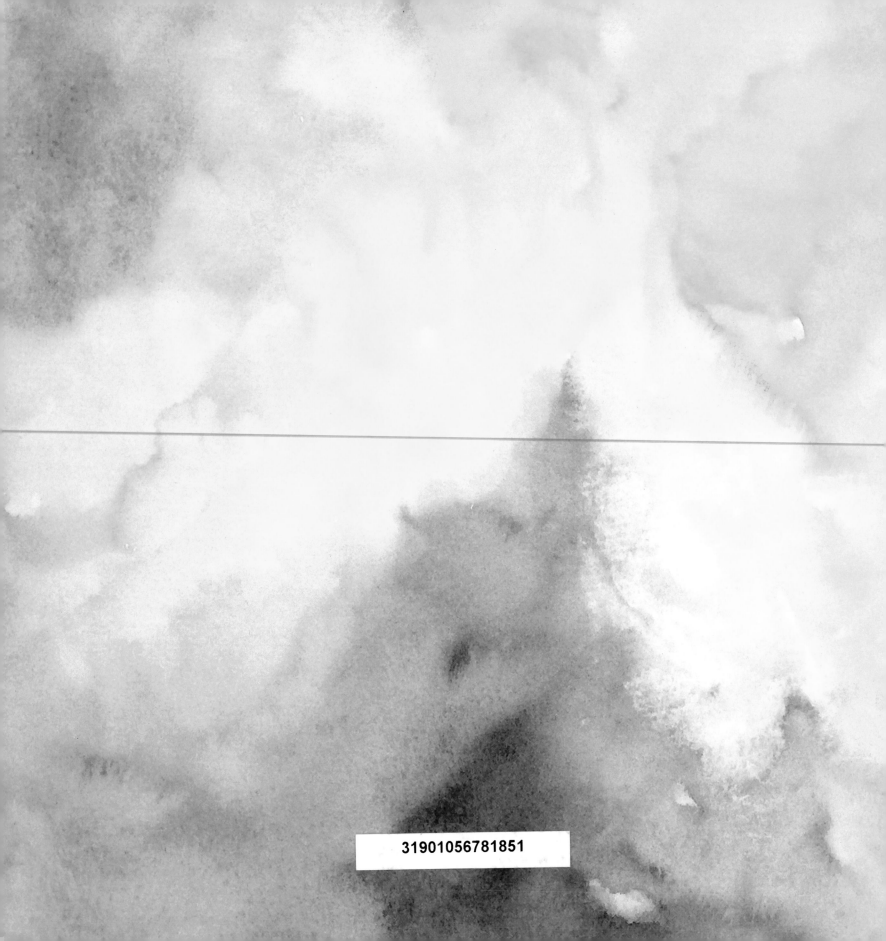